Freckleface

Julianne Moore

Strawberry

illustrated by **LeUyen Pham**

SCHOLASTIC INC.
New York Toronto London Auckland Sydney
Mexico City New Delhi Hong Kong Buenos Aires

ISBN-13: 978-0-545-08932-6
ISBN-10: 0-545-08932-8

Text copyright © 2007 by Julianne Moore.
Illustrations copyright © 2007 by LeUyen Pham. All rights reserved.
Published by Scholastic Inc., 557 Broadway, New York, NY 10012, by arrangement with
Bloomsbury Children's Books USA. SCHOLASTIC and associated logos are trademarks
and/or registered trademarks of Scholastic Inc.

12 11 10 9 8   10 11 12 13/0

Printed in the U.S.A.   40

First Scholastic printing, May 2008

Typeset in Bodoni Six Book and Minya Nouvelle
Illustrations rendered with a Japanese brush pen and digitally colored
Book design by Donna Mark

To Cal and Liv—
my own little, not-so-freckled
strawberries
—J. M.

To Melanie—
a constant happy spot in my life
—L. P.

Once upon a time there was a little girl who was just like everybody else.

She was seven.

Look! I lost
another tooth!

She was short.

She could ride a bike.

She was just like everybody else
except for one thing.

She had red hair.

And something worse . . .

FRECKLES!

How she got them was a mystery.

Her father didn't have freckles.
Her mother didn't have freckles.
Her sister didn't have freckles.

Her baby brother—
oh, yeah. He had freckles,
but he was just a baby.

People always had something to say
about her freckles.

But most of the time
they just said:

Freckleface Strawberry!

Freckleface Strawberry felt really bad.
She needed to get rid of her freckles fast.

She tried scrubbing them.

Get out of
the bathroom!

She tried lemon juice.

You smell funny.

She even tried markers,
but her mom got mad.

Nothing worked.

If she couldn't make her freckles go away,
she would just have to hide.

It worked!
All her freckles were gone.

It worked so well, she started wearing it to school.

It worked so well, nobody said anything
about her freckles anymore.

It worked so well, none of her friends
knew where she was.

Have you seen her?

She's short, and she
can ride a bike.

She has freckles
all over her body.

Freckleface Strawberry
was kind of sad. And hot.
And a little itchy.

After school, at the playground, she was lonely.
Everybody was playing except for Freckleface
Strawberry. She was sitting in the shade
wishing she wasn't so hot.

Somebody tugged on her shirt.

Mama!

It was a baby. Freckleface
Strawberry knew about babies
because of her little brother.

The baby started to laugh.

She laughed and laughed and laughed.

She was just glad she wasn't so hot anymore.
Or itchy.

Suddenly Freckleface Strawberry
heard some familiar voices:

Freckleface Strawberry,
go down the slide with me!

Freckleface Strawberry,
you have to meet the new girl.
She wears a ski mask all the time.

Freckleface Strawberry,
were you sick?

Freckleface Strawberry, we missed you!

Freckleface Strawberry smiled so wide,
she thought she would crack open.

She wasn't hot.
She wasn't itchy.
And she wasn't sad anymore.

Who cared about having a million freckles
when she had a million friends?

And maybe that mom was right and
her freckles would go away a little.

And Freckleface Strawberry really was like
everybody else—she grew up.

And her freckles . . .

But somehow, she didn't care so much after all.

In fact, she lived happily ever after.